P9-BYB-779

Betty & Veronica's Guide to Life

By Jasmine Jones

miramax books

HYPERION
New York

The "ARCHIE" property and associated character names and likenesses TM and © Archie Comic Publications, Inc., 2004, and are used under license by Diamond Select Toys and Collectibles, LLC.
All rights reserved.

The original ARCHIE characters were conceived by John Goldwater and drawn by Bob Montana for Archie Comics.

Visit BETTY & VERONICA® online at
www.archiecomics.com

Volo® is a registered trademark of Disney Enterprises, Inc.
No part of this book may be reproduced or transmitted in any form or by any means, electronic or mechanical, including photocopying, recording, or by any information storage and retrieval system, without written permission from the publisher.
For information address Hyperion Books for Children,
114 Fifth Avenue, New York, New York 10011-5690.

Printed in Singapore
First Edition
1 3 5 7 9 10 8 6 4 2

This book is set in 13-point Cheltenham.
ISBN 0-7868-5567-3

Visit www.hyperionbooksforchildren.com

Dear Reader,

What are the essentials that a girl needs to know in order to turn heads, have a fabulous wardrobe, spend time with great friends, and sail through school? The secrets are all here! For the first time ever, I'm handing out the 411 for living life, Ronnie style. Oh, and Betty threw in a few ideas, too. Hope you love my book!

Kisses and hugs,
Veronica

Hi, Reader!

Um . . . I think that Veronica is *trying* to say that, even though she and I are totally different, we've been best friends for years. And, let's face it, our differences are what keep things interesting. That's what made us decide to write this *Guide to Life*. Whether you're sweet or sophisticated, this guide will show you what you need to set yourself apart and show the world who you are. Get ready to unlock the secrets to your own fabulous style! I know we're going to have fun.

Friends forever,
Betty

Dating

Choose Your Perfect Guy Type!

Let's face it, there are way too many guys out there, and too little time to enjoy them! You need to target your perfect crush. What's your type? Check the list below, and see what you like!

The Strong, Silent Type

Some girls love a guy with big muscles. An active guy is perfect for a girl who loves sports and spending time outdoors. (Just make sure your crush's bicep isn't bigger than his brain!) Of course, this kind of boy isn't really *my* style. Sure, it can be fun to watch a guy when he's making tackles on the football field, but—personally—I don't like it when boys spend more time at practice than with me!

The Prankster

Dating a funny guy can be loads of fun. If you love to check out hilarious movies and laugh until tears stream down your face, this is your guy. He's into making jokes and pulling pranks . . . as long as nobody gets hurt, of course. What*ever*. To each her own. But any guy who thinks that a whoopee cushion is the world's greatest Valentine's Day gift is automatically off my list.

The Individualist

If you hate following the crowd, this is your type. He doesn't care what others think and marches to the beat of a different drummer. The two of you will have fun talking about things that only you understand and spending time doing exactly as you both please—without caring whether it's "cool" or not.

The Intellectual

There are plenty of guys out there who have major-league minds. Dating a brainiac can be a blast if you enjoy going out to museums, hanging at the library, or staring up at the stars. Plus, you'll have a built-in study partner. And what parent can argue with that?

The Sophisticate

What girl doesn't love a guy with excellent manners and perfect taste? Archie's cousin Alistair is like that—and he's completely dreamy! He's just like Archie . . . if Archie never forgot your birthday, showed up late, spent time with other girls, drove your father crazy, or spent all afternoon eating burgers with Jughead!

The All-American Boy

Sigh! What girl's heart doesn't go pitter-pat when it comes to a sweet guy like this one? Okay, so maybe he isn't all that rich or incredibly sophisticated . . . but a guy who's cute, smart, and totally thoughtful is hard to come by! When you find one, dig in your claws, and don't let go!

Catching His Eye

Sometimes, you want to let a guy know that you're interested without being totally, well, OBVIOUS! But how can you let a guy know that you exist without shouting, "Um . . . hel-*lo*? Yoo-hoo! I'm over here, Mr. Crush-Boy!" Here are a few things that have worked for me. . . .

🦋 **Think Pink!** Or blue, or purple, or yellow, or orange . . . a little flash of color can sometimes work wonders for getting attention. If your clothes tend to fade into the background, you might want to try something bright for a change. You could also borrow a piece of pretty jewelry (I like to borrow my sister's), a cool hat, or a funky bag—anything new and noteworthy. You might find yourself collecting phone numbers along with those compliments!

🦋 **Don't Fake It.** If you don't know a free throw from a fadeaway, don't pretend that you're the biggest Lakers fan on the planet just to talk to your basketball-loving crush! The same goes for music, books, or movies. At best, you'll find yourself spending time doing things that you hate—and, at worst, you'll look like a big phony! But if you have different tastes, it's cool to trade notes on what each of you likes. Don't be afraid to try something new—if you love Mozart and your guy is into Good Charlotte, maybe you can suggest swapping MP3s so that you can check out what he's raving about. Just don't pretend to be an expert on something you're not. (Take it from me: Veronica once tried to impress guys by winning a surfing contest with a remote-controlled surfboard . . . and things got ugly pretty fast!)

🦋 **Go with What You Know.** You and your guy probably already have something in common—maybe it's a class, hobby, or an after-school activity. If you know that you and your crush have a shared interest, make it work for you. Ask if he wants to get together to tackle that science project, study for that test, play tennis, or whatever! (Bonus: two minds are better than one . . . especially when it comes to school projects.)

Work Your Skills. What are you good at? Whether your thing is acting, singing, dancing, painting, playing sports, or writing, make sure Crush-Boy has a chance to see you shine. If you whip up cupcakes for the big bake sale, give him a taste! Or, if you have a drawing in the art show, point it out! I know, I know . . . sometimes it's hard to toot your own horn. That's when you have to get your friends to help! If your best bud knows about your crush, maybe she can toot away for you. After all, what are friends for?

What to Do When Your Guy Needs a Makeover

Let's face it, there are some guys out there who are kind of . . . challenged in the appearance department. How do you turn your oh-so-sweet but only so-so-looking guy into a major dreamboat? Let's take a careful look at the situation.

BRAIN FILLED WITH BORING FACTS

NERD-STYLE GLASSES

PUNY MUSCLES

KNOBBY KNEES

NERDY SHOES—UGH!

GORGEOUS
EYES

BRAIN FILLED WITH
THOUGHTS OF YOU

BULGING
BICEPS!

KILLER
LEGS

COOL SHOES!

How do you turn a nerd into a superhunk? It's very simple. Just make the nerd disappear!

Just kidding!

Betty's List of Dos

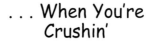

. . . When You're
Crushin'

[✔] **Do** wear clothes that are pretty but make you feel comfortable. You won't be able to chat Mr. Wonderful up if your pants are so tight that you can't breathe!

[✔] **Do** smile, smile, smile! Everybody—guys included—loves people who are friendly and fun to be around.

[✔] **Do** spend time getting to know your guy. It is much easier to turn a guy friend into a boyfriend than to make a boyfriend out of someone you don't even know.

[✔] **Do** let him know that you think you have interests in common, and that you'd love to spend time together doing what you both enjoy!

Veronica's List of Don'ts

> . . . When You're Crushin'

[✔] **Don't** forget to dress to impress. You don't want him to see you in some old rag that you've worn a bunch of times before, do you?

[✔] **Don't** let him think you're too available. Send yourself flowers from a "secret admirer" on Valentine's Day and/or your birthday. Get those jealousy juices flowing in your guy!

[✔] **Don't** join some boring after-school club just because you want to spend time with a particular guy. There are loads of fish in the sea—you don't want to get stuck swimming in one small pond!

[✔] **Don't** spend too much time chatting with a guy on the phone. After ten minutes, pretend that your call-waiting has just beeped, and tell him that you have to go. You want to let him know that you're in demand!

Veronica's First Date Checklist

Okay, he's cute, seems sweet, and has asked you out on a date. But does he pass the test?

❏ Did he arrive on time?

❏ Was he dressed neatly, with hair combed?

❏ Did he bring a gift—like flowers, candy, or a diamond necklace?

❏ Did he chat nicely with your 'rents?

❏ Did he compliment your outfit?

❏ Did he open the car door for you?

❏ Did he take you somewhere special?

❏ Did he keep his eyes on you—and off other girls—the whole time?

Take it from me, girls—if a boy misses more than two on the list, don't bother going out with him on Date Number Two. Toss him back!

Betty Explains It All

How to Turn Your Guy Friend into Something More

1. Have you been trying to think up ways to spend extra time with your best guy friend lately?

Take this quiz.

2. When you know you're going to see him, do you spend five times longer than usual in the bathroom getting ready?

3. Does every single thing in the world remind you of your guy friend?

4. Do your girlfriends tell you that you talk about him *waaaay* too much?

5. Does everyone think you're a couple?

If you answered yes to any of these questions, you may be crushing on your guy friend! Believe me, I know what that's like. But what can you do to let him know that you're really interested?

Here are a few ideas:

🌊 **Get him alone.** Do you usually hang with this guy in a group of friends? If so, it's normal that

he would see you as one of the gang. Why not suggest that the two of you do something that you would normally do in a group—get pizza, catch a movie, snag a smoothie— as a twosome. Spending time with you alone might help him see you in a whole new light.

🌊 **Get your friends to help.** If your friends are willing, ask them to find out if this guy is interested in anyone else . . . and if he isn't, maybe they can suggest *you* as the perfect girl!

Snag him as a study partner. Mmmm, all of those quiet evenings poring over algebra equations . . . Okay, so maybe it isn't the most romantic setting, but at least you'll be spending time alone together!

Be direct! Hey, the twentieth century is *over*—there's no point in acting coy and waiting around for him to ask you out. If you want to turn him from friend-boy into boyfriend, *ask* him! Even if he says that he wants to keep it on the friendship side, you'll know where you stand.

Veronica's Top Ten Tips For a Perfect Date

Here they
are. . . .

1. Always start by looking your best. Be sure to budget at least three hours for your manicure, pedicure, facial treatment, and hairstyle. Hey, it takes dedication to look this good!

2. Dress appropriately. You don't want to wear a miniskirt if you're going bowling.

3. Make sure you've got the right guy. Hey—I know some girls hate to spend a Saturday night alone, but I'd rather sit home solo than go out with Mr. Wrong.

4. Always bring extra money, just in case. You never know when you might have to storm out—like if your guy looks at another girl, for example!

5. Don't let your friends know where you're headed. You never know when they'll pop up and surprise you—turning a romantic twosome into a noisy eightsome!

6. If you're going out for dinner, avoid messy pasta dishes. You don't want to end up with half of your dinner in your lap!

7. Let your guy know that hanging out with his buddies and watching the game on TV is not a date. You don't want a bunch of rowdy guys spilling pizza and soda on your clothes after you just spent three hours getting ready, do you?

8. Never let the boy pick the movie. Unless you like watching things blow up.

9. A picnic may seem romantic, but make sure that you bring plenty of bug spray. The problem with nature is that there are tons of creepy-crawlies out there! (Not to mention dirt . . .)

10. When your guy comes to the door, try not to let your dad answer it. Otherwise, it'll be five hours of the third degree— and, if your dad is like mine, and your guy is like Archie—you may not get to go out at all!

Betty & Veronica's Guide to Boyfriend Boot Camp

Boys need plenty of training in order to grow into proper, loyal boyfriends.

There are a few basic principles that go a long way toward making you guy into someone utterly datable.

♡ **Boyfriends should be well groomed at all times.**

Don't be afraid to ask him to toss out that old holey, smelly T-shirt that he loves to play football in. And feel free to make some adjustments to his hairstyle. Boys have trouble keeping themselves clean—they will appreciate the attention.

♡ Boyfriends need to be fed a steady diet containing the four basic food groups: burgers, fries, pizza, and ice cream.
Feel free to offer your boy a special treat, such as a homemade brownie or chocolate-chip cookie, as a reward for good behavior.

♡ Boyfriends need plenty of exercise.
I find that the mall is a great place for a boyfriend workout. Trotting into stores after you is excellent as cardio, and carrying your heavy packages builds strong muscles.

♡ Remember that a boyfriend always appreciates a smile and a pat.
He needs to hear "good boy" on occasion . . . like when he has brought you an expensive gift. (Very good boy!)

School

Teachers

Teachers have the power to make your day great—or a total disaster. Take a look at your schedule and see if you have to deal with any of the types below. Then read on to see how to deal with them . . . it'll make your life a whole lot easier!

The Terminator

This type likes rules—and likes to enforce them! If they tell you not to write in purple ink, then for goodness' sake, DON'T! You don't want to end up with a zero on a major paper just because you wanted to try out your new glitter pen. With this type, it's best to follow every rule to a T—and mind your p's and q's.

The Disorganizer

This is everyone's favorite teacher. She lets you watch films in class if they relate to what you are studying and often comes up with creative class assignments. The downside: she just might lose your midterms. With this type of teacher, it's best to keep a copy of all of your assignments, especially reports. You don't want to have to do the work all over again.

The Cheerleader

Whenever you get back your papers, they have "Excellent!" scrawled at the top—even when the grade says C–. This type of teacher loves to hand out the encouragement, and is always trying to encourage students to get involved in school activities. If you want to stay on his good side, you'd better sign up for the bake sale. This type of teacher always knows it when you haven't been showing your school spirit.

The Neat Freak

She spends an entire class period telling you how *not* to staple a paper. This type of teacher values form as much as function. The next time you have to hand in a paper, wow her with a cool cover page and a neatly handwritten or typed report. Neat freaks give extra points for style!

The Pushover

When you have tests and papers in every class on your schedule, you can always count on this teacher to give you an extension. He's equally lenient when it comes to homework—you know he'll take any excuse, as long as it's one you haven't used before. The trouble with this kind of teacher is that it's easy to let the work slide . . . until you realize that you have two papers and fifteen homework assignments to catch up on at the end of the term!

The Autobiographer

You always find his class interesting—because he's usually telling you about the crazy things he did in college or the funny thing that happened on his last camping trip. His social studies lectures turn into personal histories the minute the first person asks a question. My only tip for dealing with this type: when he goes off on some trip down memory lane about his Aunt Martha, don't ask if that story is going to be on the final.

Veronica's Locker Dos and Don'ts

Lockers can be a problem—especially when they're small and cramped. That's why I had Daddy buy me an extra-wide jumbo locker—and add a wing to the school where it would fit. Here are a few tips for those of you stuck with the usual size:

The DO locker has:

❀ A mirror for makeup checks

❀ A brush and a few accessories—for gym or a plain old bad hair day

❀ Books and notebooks color-coded by subject . . . and assembled to look like a rainbow

❀ Pictures of friends and dream boys—real or imaginary

❀ A pencil bag or box stuffed with things you might need for studying—sticky notes, highlighters, and index cards for handing out your number to cute guys in the library

✱ A small sack under the top vents to catch the notes your friends slip into your locker between classes

The DON'T locker has:

✱ A three-month-old bag lunch buried beneath your history book

✱ Medals and ribbons from every mathlete tournament and spelling bee you've ever won, so that everyone at school will know that you're the BEST

✱ Giant photographs of yourself glued inside

✱ Your stuffed-animal collection, taking up the space where your books are supposed to be

✱ Seven "World's Greatest Teacher" mugs—which you plan to give to each of your teachers for Christmas—on the top shelf

✱ A gym bag full of stinky sweats that you've been "forgetting" for the past six weeks to take home to wash

School Spirit

We've got spirit, yes, we do!

Betty's Top Five Tips for Showing Your School Spirit

1. Run for student council! It's a great way to get to know the different kids in your class and find out what their concerns are!

2. Join an athletic team. It's fun, and it's great exercise!

3. Participate in school fund-raisers, like candy sales and car washes. You'll show others how much your school means to you, and it can pay off in big cash for fun activities!

4. Organize a school party or other event. It can be a great way to get people to work together, while expressing your creativity!

5. Support your cheerleaders by giving them a holler at the pep rally! (Or just cheer like crazy if you're already one of them.)

It's important to get behind your school—your individual contributions make it a better place for everyone.

Veronica's Top Five Tips for Showing Your School Spirit

1. Be sure to attend all of your school's basketball games ... and any other sport featuring guys in shorts.

2. Make a contribution to the bake sale. (The last time they had one, I contributed a dollar, and they gave me two chocolate-chip cookies and a Rice Krispie treat!)

3. Join your school's dance committee. That way you can make sure that the theme is more like "Moonlight in Venice" and less like "Professional Wrestler Rumble-Mania."

4. Make sure the football players know that you support them by lavishing attention on them whenever you get a chance.

5. Try to remember how to spell the name of your school. It makes all of those "Give me an *e!*" cheers *so* much easier.

Favorite Subject

Now it's time to talk about my favorite school subject—lunch!

There are lots of ways to spend your hour besides just downing the latest meat loaf special. First of all, I always save a table for my best buds. Lunch just isn't lunch if you don't spend it with people you like! Here are a few games we like to play in the lunchroom:

Hottie-Spotting

Which of your girlfriends can find the absolute cutest guy in the lunchroom? You'll have fun trying! (I have to admit I have a natural skill for this game—it's one of my favorites.)

Tater Tot Tic-Tac-Toe

Fun for two players: one person dips her Tater Tots in ketchup, the other leaves hers plain. Set up a French-fry tic-tac-toe board and play. The winner gets the fries and the Tater Tots! (*And* the glory.)

What's-on-the-Menu Twenty Questions

Have you ever looked down at the food on your tray and thought, What is that stuff? Then this game is for you! Try to guess what the dish is supposed to be, then elect a volunteer to ask the lunch-line lady if you're right. The winner gets a dollar to go buy a candy bar from the vending machine.

How Many Burgers Can Jughead Eat?

This is really more of a spectator sport—but it's fun to watch. I have my friends guess ahead of time how many burgers Jughead will down before the bell rings. Extra points if he sets a new personal best!

One thing that's hard about high school is that kids like to hang out in little groups of friends called cliques instead of everyone just being friendly and chilling together.

Sigh. But still, it's a fact of life. Where do you and your friends stand when it comes to cliques? Here's how to spot the typical types in any school:

Do your friends have:

☆ Bulging muscles?

☆ An after-school schedule packed with sports?

☆ Pennants and/or trophies in their rooms?

☆ A hundred pairs of shorts?

If you said yes to three or more of these questions, your friends are jocks. Athletes can be a lot of fun, especially if you're the type of person who loves to spend time outdoors exercising. Also, people who play team sports tend to know a lot about working together. Besides, if you ever need help lifting something heavy, these are your go-to peeps.

Do your friends have:

☆ More than one calculator?

☆ A book bag that feels like a sack of lead?

☆ A collection of sci-fi DVDs?

☆ A schedule packed with honors classes?

☆ A membership card for the Junior Engineering and Technological Society?

Yes to three or more of these questions means that your friends are brains! Congratulations—you guys probably have the highest combined GPA in the school. You never have to worry about tests or grades, because you like studying . . . and you always come out tops in the class!

Do your friends have:

☆ A ton of friends?

☆ The latest fashions?

☆ A mega-long IM buddy list?

☆ A closet bigger than the storeroom at Wal-Mart?

☆ A weekend schedule packed with parties?

☆ The numbers of their hairstylists programmed into their speed dials?

Four or more yes answers means that your friends rule the school when it comes to cool. They set the fashion trends and throw all the best parties. They're the social butterflies, whom everyone wants to hang with—and they always look good! (Sound familiar, Veronica?) If you love fashion, shopping, and going to parties, this is your crowd.

Do your friends have:
☆ A new trauma every day?
☆ Funky clothes that they bought at vintage stores?
☆ The lead in the school play?
☆ All three *Lord of the Rings* scripts committed to memory?
☆ Notebooks full of poetry they're working on?
☆ More black in their wardrobe than a cat burglar?

Three or more yes answers means that your buds are dramaramas. Creative and quirky, this crowd is always scoring big points for originality. If you're seriously into the arts—acting, singing, dancing, music, writing, or painting—you're probably hanging with these guys.

But what if you have a few friends who fit into one group and a few who fit into another and some who don't fit into any group at all? Take me, for example. My friends include Veronica (a social butterfly), Moose (an athlete), Dilton (a mathlete), and Jughead (who knows?). I don't like to hang with any single type of person. I guess you could call me a chameleon. I like to play sports and fix cars, but sometimes I like to go shopping and look pretty, too. I can be social, but I can also be studious. And that's okay. You don't have to fit into one group to have a bunch of different friends. Actually, it can be the best way to find the greatest gang in the world!

My parents are always asking me why I need to chat on the phone with my friends all night if I've just spent all day seeing them at school. Why, we're talking about what we did that day, of course! It's important to keep in touch on a daily, if not hourly, basis, so Ronnie and I have worked up a few ideas for those of you who understand the need to reach out to your friends.

Everyone loves to get notes in their lockers. But nobody likes reading a dull letter with no pizzazz. How can you make your notes the hottest ticket in school? Read on!

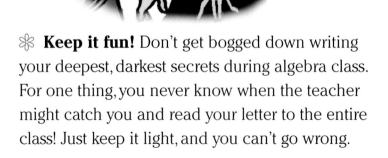

❋ **Keep it fun!** Don't get bogged down writing your deepest, darkest secrets during algebra class. For one thing, you never know when the teacher might catch you and read your letter to the entire class! Just keep it light, and you can't go wrong.

✳ **Don't talk about how bored you are.** Let's face it, a note about being bored is boring. Period. If you're stuck in a class and the teacher is droning on and on about something you've heard a hundred times, write about something else—like cool weekend plans, or the upcoming football game.

✳ **Fold 'em up!** Half the fun of getting a note is unwrapping it like an awesome present! It's easy to download origami instructions—next time, try folding your note like a butterfly, frog, or crane!

✳ **Add art.** A note is more fun when it comes with illustrations. If you're writing about summer vacation plans, add a picture of yourself and your BFF under a beach umbrella, or paddling in a canoe. It's a great way to make a blah note look fun!

Hey, Veronica,

Want to go to Pop's after school today? I hear he has a new milk shake flavor—Wildberry Supreme—that I'm dying to try! I can meet you at your locker, and we can go from there.

Ugh! I'm totally swamped with a pile of reading for English. Have you finished *To Kill a Mockingbird* yet? Oh, wait—don't tell me. I don't want to know if the mockingbird dies at the end!

Gotta go. Bell is about to ring. Write back and let me know about Pops!

XOXO,
Betty

Best-Friend Blues!

Dear Betty,
    Sometimes my best friend says mean things about me behind my back, and the other day, she announced the name of my crush to everyone in our class! When it's just me and her, we have a lot of fun, but I don't like it when she's mean. What should I do?
                                        Signed,
                                        Bothered in Boston

Dear Bothered,
    Hmmm . . . it sounds like your best friend needs some lessons in friendship! Real friends don't talk meanly about each other, and they don't give up secrets. Maybe your friend doesn't realize that she's hurting your feelings. Talk to her one on one, and tell her that the things she is doing upset you. If she doesn't change, it may be time to start focusing on your other friendships—I'm sure that someone else will treat you the way you deserve to be treated!

                                        Love,
                                        Betty

Dear Betty,

My best friend has started hanging out with another girl from her ballet class all of the time. Sometimes they ask me to come along, but sometimes they don't. Even when I sit with them at lunch, they're always talking about the girls in ballet, whom I don't know. What can I do to make my best friend pay attention to me again?

Signed,
Alone in Arizona

Dear Alone,

I don't know if ballet is your thing, but have you considered joining their class? It might give you an opportunity to spend more time with your friend and get to know the new girl better. If that won't work, try inviting your best friend out for things the two of you enjoy. You don't have to wait around for her to invite you along when she goes out with her other friend!

Love,
Betty

Dear Betty,

My best friend and I are crushing on the same guy. Sometimes he seems to like me better, but sometimes he pays more attention to her. It seems like my friend and I are always arguing over this boy! What can I do?

Signed,

Jealous in Dallas

Dear Jealous,

Gee, this sounds familiar! I don't have too much advice for you on this subject. If the guy won't commit to either one of you, maybe you should start looking elsewhere. (Easier said than done, I know!) Just remember that friendship is the most important thing. No guy—no matter how cute, thoughtful, or freckled he is—should be able to come between best friends!

Love,

Betty

Anatomy of a Best Friend

"The world's greatest friend" has a lot of wonderful qualities. Does your BFF have what it takes to be a perfect bud for life? Check the chart to find out!

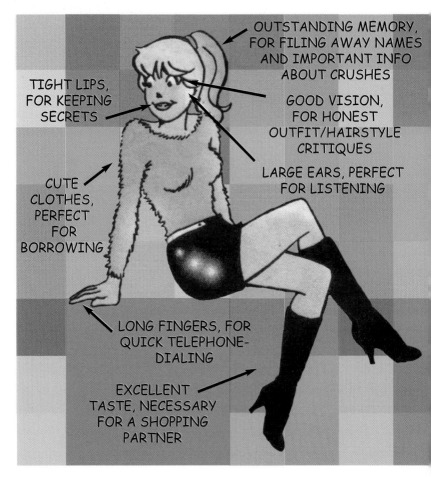

OUTSTANDING MEMORY, FOR FILING AWAY NAMES AND IMPORTANT INFO ABOUT CRUSHES

TIGHT LIPS, FOR KEEPING SECRETS

GOOD VISION, FOR HONEST OUTFIT/HAIRSTYLE CRITIQUES

CUTE CLOTHES, PERFECT FOR BORROWING

LARGE EARS, PERFECT FOR LISTENING

LONG FINGERS, FOR QUICK TELEPHONE-DIALING

EXCELLENT TASTE, NECESSARY FOR A SHOPPING PARTNER

Friendship Is a Two-Way Street

Veronica and I have a lot in common. We both love cute clothes and cute boys—especially Archie! But even though we usually get along great, there are times when Ronnie and I don't get along so well. Like the time I lost a bet, and she forced me to be her maid for a day. How do I stay friends with someone so . . . challenging?

Betty's Tips for Staying Friends with Veronica

1. Just accept the fact that I'll never be as well dressed as she is . . . no matter how much money I spend.
2. Never let her talk me into cleaning her room.
3. Spend as much time as possible at the mall or by the pool—places that bring out the best in Veronica's personality.
4. Never let her know when I'm hanging with Archie!
5. Don't plan anything outdoorsy with Veronica, especially if it involves getting dirty.
6. Don't expect Ronnie to pay attention to the movie when cute boys are in the theater.
7. Expect to hear all about fabulous trips!

8. Accept the fact that Veronica turns heads wherever she goes.

9. If Ronnie ever gives me a fashion tip, take it! (Unless I'm going out with Archie . . . in which case she might give me bad advice!)

10. Remember to wear comfortable shoes for long treks through her closet!

The Top Five Things That Drive Me Crazy About My Best Friend, Betty Cooper

1. She's good at *everything*—she gets an A in science, works at her after-school job, and fixes Archie's car!

2. Blondes have more fun.

3. She never lets her hair down.

4. Archie always wants to study with *her* instead of me—just because she's a straight-A student!

5. She never says anything mean about anyone—even when they really deserve it. (It makes me look bad!)

Betty and I have been friends forever! Betty is sweet, fun-loving, patient, and kind. But let's face it, sometimes that Goody Two-shoes act can get really annoying. Oh, sure. She's my best friend. But even best friends can drive each other crazy!

Fighting with Your Best Bud

Arguing is part of what friends do. But making up can be hard to do after a major blowup. If you end up on the wrong side of a friendsplosion, here are some creative ways to tell your best bud that you're sorry.

🍀 **Make it musical.** Write a song, and leave it on her answering machine. The sillier the better! When she stops laughing, she'll have to forgive you.

🍀 **Get things cookin'.** Bake a batch of her favorite brownies or cookies. Use a small tube of colored frosting to decorate the treats with the words *I'm sorry*, then head over to her house. Sometimes, all it takes is something sweet to wash the bitterness away.

🍀 **You've got mail.** Get out the old construction paper, doilies, and scissors to make your best bud a valentine . . . even if it's the middle of July. Be sure to let her know how much your friendship means to you, then slip the card into her mailbox.

🍀 **Clip coupons.** Use paper or your computer to make your friend an "I'm Sorry" coupon, good for one free makeup smoothie or ice cream cone at her favorite place. Redeemable only if she forgives you completely!

It can also be a good idea to say that you're sorry that you argued *even if you still think you were right*. Sometimes it's worth it to agree to disagree if it means saving your friendship!

The Anti-Friends

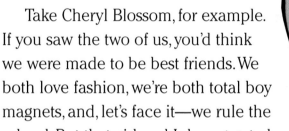

> I've had my share of enemies. Sometimes they're jealous of my clothes, or of my fabulous house, or even of the time I spend with Archiekins.

Take Cheryl Blossom, for example. If you saw the two of us, you'd think we were made to be best friends. We both love fashion, we're both total boy magnets, and, let's face it—we rule the school. But that girl and I do *not* get along . . . and sometimes we spend our time dreaming up ways to try to make each other miserable. It's called payback.

But it could be worse. Enemies come in all different styles. Below are some of the kinds I've seen, and suggestions for how to cope:

☆ **The bully.** Every school has one—a person who likes to push other people around. If you're dealing with someone who makes physical threats, talk to a teacher or trusted adult immediately. Don't worry about how it will look, just let someone know that this person might get physical. At least someone will be watching and will understand if you have to defend yourself.

The rival. You got a 95 on the math test, she got a 97. You got tickets to a cool concert, she got backstage passes. You made three assists in the soccer game, she scored two goals. This kind of enemy can drive you crazy, but she can also force you to work harder and get better. Just make sure that you don't become obsessed with beating her. Do your best, and hope that the challenges make you stronger.

The loudmouth. "Sticks and stones may break my bones, but words can never hurt me." Yeah, right. The truth is, words *can* hurt. But try to keep in mind that the problem is hers, not yours. The next time the Loudmouth starts teasing, try to imagine her as a squawking chicken, flapping her wings and letting her feathers fly. You wouldn't let a chicken bother you, right? It takes time, but if you just ignore her—the way you would a television with the sound turned off—she'll get bored and move on.

☼ **The person who dislikes you for no reason.** Ouch, this can hurt. But there will be people in this world with whom you just don't get along. It may not make sense, but there it is. Don't waste your time trying to win this person over. Just accept that not everyone can like you, and focus on spending time with the people who already do.

☼ **The backstabber.** It hurts to have a friend who turns on you, or talks about you behind your back. Try very hard to see this person for who she is. You can't trust her with secrets, so don't. Be wary, too, if she claims to have changed and wants to be your friend again. Friendship is earned, not given away for free.

Family

My Top Ten Reasons I'm Glad I'm an Only Child

1. I don't have to draw an invisible line down the center of the room when I'm mad at my imaginary sister.

2. No one tattles on me except the butler.

3. No one borrows my sweater and spills something on it, then sneaks it back into my closet without telling me.

4. No one makes faces at me at the breakfast table.

5. No one pokes me in the arm in the back of the limo.

6. I never get blamed for something I didn't do.

7. Christmas morning is all about me.

8. No one complains that I'm Daddykins's favorite—even though I am.

9. I don't have to share my clothes, my car, my room, or my vacation chalet in the Swiss Alps.

10. I always get the last cookie.

Ask Betty

Dear Betty:

I love my mom, but she's totally embarrassing! She's always trying to act "cool" around my friends. She's even started borrowing my clothes and makeup—she even bought a pair of leather pants! It would be so much better if she would just act her age. How can I make her act more like a normal mom?

Signed,
My Mom's Too Cool for School

Dear Too Cool:

I guess the question is—has your mother always acted like this? Or is her behavior new? If it's new, your mom is probably just trying to connect with you by sharing your interests. Unfortunately, her behavior isn't working. Talk to her and explain that you love her and that she doesn't have to become like your friends in order to be a good mom. However, if your mother has always been trendy, then you'll just have to accept that this is her personality, and you can't change it. But remember that almost everyone thinks that her parents are embarrassing for one reason or another. Besides, your friends should care about you—not what your mother wears or says.

Love,
Betty

Hmmm . . . reading over Veronica's list sure makes being an only child seem like fun! But I wouldn't trade my older brother, Chic, or my older sister, Polly, for the world. Growing up, I always had someone to play with. And both of them were always around to talk to when I was having problems with friends or with our parents. Okay, okay—so getting along with a brother or sister isn't always easy. (Especially when you're locked in a wrestling match over the peanut butter.) But they sure keep life interesting!

Here are a few tips for getting along with your sibs:

★ **If you're going to get into a fight with your sister or brother, try to avoid calling them names like Stink Breath, Porcupine Head, or Lima-Bean Brain.** Name-calling can be tempting when you're angry. But it will only lead to hurt feelings—and a lecture from Mom and Dad. If you're upset with your sibling, keep the conversation about what's bothering you . . . don't say something that you'll only have to apologize for later.

★ **Learn to share.** You can fight over that last cupcake—or you can split it. You can argue about whose turn it is to do the dishes—or you can volunteer to dry if your sister washes. I know, I know—sometimes life isn't fair. Sometimes you really deserve the whole cupcake. And sometimes it really isn't your turn to do the dishes. But learning to compromise and give in a little now can save you an even bigger headache later—like when your parents get involved and eat the last cupcake themselves.

★ **Say you're sorry.** If you've had an argument with your brother or sister, and you know you were wrong—don't wait! Apologize now. If you let their anger simmer, it could erupt the next time you have a disagreement over something else.

★ **Don't borrow things without permission.**
Polly and I share clothes and makeup—and we don't even have to ask each other. But in some families, this can cause some serious fights. Even if you're 99 percent sure that your sister or brother won't mind if you borrow something— ask anyway. It can't hurt.

★ **Don't hog the bathroom.** Hey—other people need to get in there! If you have to style your hair or put on makeup, set up a mirror in your bedroom. Look at it this way—at least you won't have someone distracting you from your styling routine by pounding on the door for twenty minutes.

★ **Do something fun together.** For a while, it seemed as though I only saw Polly when Mom and Dad planned activities for the whole family. I missed her, so I asked if she wanted to go shopping with me—and we had an awesome day! If you haven't been getting along with your brother or sister lately, maybe you should plan to do something you both enjoy—bake something, work on a craft project, or play a sport. That way you can spend time and remember the things you love about each other.

Betty's
Top Ten Rules for Getting Along with Parents

1. Always call home if you're going to be late. Your parents love you—don't make them worry.

2. When it comes to schoolwork, do the best you can. Good grades are important, but learning is even more important.

3. Parents are busy people—so try to pitch in and help around the house when you can.

4. If you break the rule, accept the punishment.

5. Try to see things from their point of view. Okay, so you want to stay out until three in the morning, and they want you home by eleven. Maybe it doesn't seem fair, but your ` mom and dad just want to keep you safe. Remember that and their rules will seem a lot easier to live with.

6. Remember to tell them you love them.

7. Try to use reason to get what you want. If you don't like one of your parents' rules, sit down

with them to discuss it. Maybe you can come to a compromise.

8. Never shirk chores. It just makes you look irresponsible and makes more work for your mom and dad.

9. If you think your parents might not like what you're doing, they probably won't.

10. Treat them the way you want them to treat you—with respect and love. That's what being a family's all about.

Fashion

Now, on to the most important part of this entire book—the beauty and fashion section! It doesn't take money or perfect genes to look good . . . especially if you follow the tips Betty and I have come up with!

Betty on Finding Your Signature Style

The most important thing about style is that it has to match your life. For example, I spend a lot of time outdoors, playing sports. Even though I love Ronnie's classic, sophisticated clothes, I could never expect to go snowboarding in them! That's why I stick to clothes that are stylish but comfortable, and I don't wear elaborate makeup. There are loads of girls in Riverdale, and each of them has a unique style. Check the lists below to see who you're most like!

The Girl Next Door: Betty Cooper

You're the type of girl who spends a lot of time outdoors, playing sports or doing other physical activities. You tend to favor clothes that are simple and stylish, but that keep up with your on-the-go lifestyle. No frills or ruffles, thanks. Your schedule is so jam-packed with plans and activities that you don't have time for anything fussy—*Keep It Simple* is your mantra.

When it comes to makeup, you favor a pared-down routine, with little more than lip gloss and mascara. If you're going somewhere special, add a little eyeliner (brown for fair complexions, black for darker ones) to top eyelid only, and try a lip gloss with added sparkle in a pretty shade of pink (which flatters every complexion).

Most Likely to Be in Your Closet:

Piles of comfortable jeans, flattering T-shirts, sweaters, sporty accessories

Handbag Necessities:

Lip balm, sunblock, organizer, notebook, sports sunglasses

Best Bets for Hair:

If long: Go Betty, and sweep it back in a stylish ponytail. You can jazz it up with cute, funky hair accessories, or make it look sleek by wrapping a lock of hair around the elastic and fastening it with a bobby pin beneath the ponytail so it doesn't show.

If medium: If you spend a lot of time playing sports, you won't want your hair to hang in your face. Check accessories stores for headbands, or use cute barrettes to keep stray locks out of your face.

If short: For every day, you probably want to leave your no-fuss style as is. But if you're heading out on a date or to a dance, you can dress up your look with small, sparkly barrettes or glitter gel.

The Sophisticate:
Veronica Lodge

Even if you're just headed for school, you want to look fabulous. Fashion is your passion, and you don't mind going the extra mile to look good. As long as it's in style, you're wearing it. . . . You're the kind of girl who likes to mix up her look and keep things current.

Good grooming is essential, and you'll spend whatever it takes to look your best. When it comes to makeup, you like a classic, clean look. A little red lipstick, a dash of eye shadow, and a touch of blush, and you're ready to go!

Most Likely to Be in Your Closet:

Miles and miles of fashionable clothes. Pretty, flirty tops, feminine skirts, and classic black pants are your staples. You also love shoes . . . and beauty is *waaaay* more important to you than comfort!

Handbag Necessities:

Purse-sized perfume spray, lipstick, mascara, eye shadow, and liner (for touch-ups), hairbrush, address book, cell phone, and Band-Aids, for blisters caused by those unpractical shoes

Best Bets for Hair:

If long: Classic hairstyles are your best bet. If you are headed somewhere special, experiment with a clean French twist or sleek chignon.

If medium: A classic, chin-length bob is a versatile cut that goes with just about any style. Worn down or held back with a stylish barrette, it's always a clean look.

If short: A plain, wide, black headband always looks stylish. Or jazz up short hair with eye-catching earrings.

The Glamour Queen:
Cheryl Blossom

You've got a spicy personality . . . and a wardrobe to match! You love skirts in jewel tones, eye-catching geometric prints, and flirty, feminine styles, like peasant blouses and low-slung jeans. For every day, you keep things light with brown liner, black mascara, and a dusty rose lip gloss. For evenings out, you like smoky makeup hues—dark eyeliner and gray shadow on your lids, wine or maroon tones for lips. Your hair is usually done in a fashionable but low-maintenance style—one that looks elegant even when tousled.

To brighten eyes, try a shimmering white shadow at the top of the brow bone. Also, don't forget your eyebrows! Use an eyebrow brush or a toothbrush to sweep brows into place. If you like to add sparkle, don't forget that nails can be an unexpected place to add shine! There are loads of shimmery, glittery shades to choose from.

Most Likely to Be Found in Your Closet:

Flirty, feminine skirts; well-made, classic handbags; platform shoes; wrap blouses in soft colors

Handbag Necessities:

Scented hand lotion, shimmery lip gloss, nail polish (for touch-ups), tiny pocket mirror, tortoiseshell comb

Best Bets For Hair:

If long or medium: Your stylish mane always looks great. If you're going out, try leaving a few face-framing tendrils and tucking the rest back with a few fun clips.

If short: Use styling gel to make hair supershiny, or go for a choppy look; use fingers to scrunch hair into small sections, then allow hair to set.

The Trendissima: Ginger Lopez

Your look shouts one word: FUN! You love dance and hip-hop, and you look to the streets for your style inspiration. You aren't afraid to do something wild with your hair and makeup, and you love to play with your look. You tend to wear bold prints, bright colors, and interesting fabrics . . . and you aren't afraid to shop in a vintage store or sew beads on to something to add interest. When it comes to hair and makeup, you like to switch things up with wash-out color for your bangs, glitter eye shadow, and eye-catching accessories. Your makeup bag is overflowing with vibrant colors: fuchsia for cheeks, blue for eyes, hot pink for lips, and maybe even green for nails!

Most Likely to Be in Your Closet:

Vintage clothes that you have modified yourself, tons of miniskirts, shirts in playful patterns that show off your individuality, and baskets of funky accessories

Handbag Necessities:

The latest gadgets, like cell phone or pager; a book of poetry; temporary tattoos

Best Bets for Hair:

If long: Try sweeping your mane into a messy updo, or braid sections and fasten the ends with tiny, glittery clips.

If medium or short: Don't be afraid of color! There are loads of fun temporary colors that wash out with shampoo, and you can change them to coordinate with your clothes.

Veronica's
Basic Beauty Don'ts

Don't answer the door wearing a facial mask.

Don't forget to put a top coat on your nails for extra shine and strength.

Don't try for a "more intense color" by leaving hair dye in for an extra thirty minutes.

Don't skip the sunblock in an effort to look tan for the school dance, unless, of course, your dress goes well with red!

Betty's Organized Closet

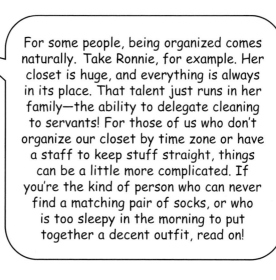

For some people, being organized comes naturally. Take Ronnie, for example. Her closet is huge, and everything is always in its place. That talent just runs in her family—the ability to delegate cleaning to servants! For those of us who don't organize our closet by time zone or have a staff to keep stuff straight, things can be a little more complicated. If you're the kind of person who can never find a matching pair of socks, or who is too sleepy in the morning to put together a decent outfit, read on!

Buy clothes in coordinating colors. If most of your clothes go together, you won't have to think too hard about how to put together an outfit. I like clothes in solid colors—that way, I never have to worry about patterns or stripes clashing. Ronnie likes to pair blouses with black pants or skirts, but I mostly have to make sure that any tops I buy go well with jeans.

When in doubt, toss it out! Getting rid of
extra clothing makes space for the things you're
using. Go through your closet and be honest with
yourself about what you really wear. If you haven't
worn something in over a year, most likely it isn't
going to become your favorite item overnight.
Convince your parents to hold a tag sale (a great
way to earn extra money!), or donate unused and
outgrown clothes to charity. Another idea would
be to call your friends and organize a clothing
swap. Everyone gets together and puts out a few
nice things that they just don't wear, and then
exchanges each item for something new,

contributed by someone else. It's like going shopping—for free! Any leftover clothes can be given away.

Separate by season. Hey—what's that giant down vest doing hogging prime real estate in the middle of your closet in July? Spring and fall are seasons for making space. Once the weather turns chilly, move your lightweight clothes to the back of your closet, or fold up your shorts, breezy skirts, and tank tops, and put them in a box marked SUMMER. At the end of winter, have your sweaters cleaned, and then put them away with the rest of your heavy clothes. You'll find what you need for the moment much faster!

Hang like with like. If you spend twenty minutes every morning flipping through hangers trying to find your cute denim skirt, you need to reorganize! Put clothes you don't use very often (party dresses) in the far left of your closet (if right-handed; otherwise, organize in the opposite direction!). Then follow with more casual dresses, skirts, blouses, pants, jeans, and casual tops.

Keep accessories tidy. Belts can be rolled up and placed in a drawer, or hung from a hook on the inside door or outside wall of your closet. Purses and bags are easy to find if you put them in baskets or on shelves in your closet. A hat collection looks supercute hung from hooks on the wall.

Keep socks away from the dryer monster.

Okay, if you're like me, you have a huge collection of single socks, which, let's face it, isn't that useful—unless you're into making sock puppets. I have two tips that can help you find a pair when you need it. Buy socks all in one color or style. I have two kinds of socks: black (to wear with school clothes) and white (for sports). All of my black socks are the same, and so are all of my white socks. That way, I don't have to worry about matching! And pin pairs together before you toss them in the wash. Keep a small bag of safety pins near your laundry basket, and each night when you get undressed, make sure that your pair is clipped together. Bonus: you don't have to sort socks when the laundry is done!

Veronica's Top Ten Fashion Tips

1. You can always jazz up a ho-hum outfit with a cute accessory on your arm. My favorite is named Archie.

2. If it's on sale, buy two!

3. Brave generals and fearless shoppers always shout, "Charge!"

4. Daddies are there to pay, never to choose.

5. They can't kick you out of the mall until all the stores are closed.

6. There is no such thing as too stylish.

7. Fashion is like a boy—you have to pay attention, or you could be left behind!

8. No outfit is complete until it is accessorized!

9. Don't be too hard on your tresses (with blow dryers, curling irons, or color treatments) or it'll be, "Hair today, gone tomorrow"!

10. When you're not sure what to wear, always skirt the issue!

Health

Eating Healthfully and Exercising

Let's face it—it's hard to have fun when you aren't feeling well. A great body is one that is fit and lets you do the things you want to do.

That's why i so important take good ca of your bod After all, it the only on you've got! Here are a f tips for keep yourself in tip-top shap

Eat plenty of fruits and veggies. Fruits and vegetables provide the fiber and vitamins you need for a healthy body. The government suggests that you get five servings a day. What's a serving? A single apple, half a banana, a cup of greens— in general, an amount that's roughly the size of a baseball. If you have a sliced banana on your cereal in the morning, carrot sticks for a snack at lunch, and a normal-sized salad along with dinner, you'll have eaten your five servings for the day. Bonus: fruits and veggies are low in calories and help to fill you up!

Balance, balance, balance! Remember the five food groups? Try to make sure that you're eating from two or more at every meal. Think about a plate. If one fourth of the plate has protein (meat, eggs, dairy), one fourth has grains (bread, pasta, cereal), and one half has fruits and vegetables, you'll be eating a well-balanced meal.

Don't follow fad diets—use your head! There are a lot of crazy diets out there—some of which tell you to eat only one kind of food or to limit severely your calorie intake. These diets can be hard to follow and worse, dangerous. If you're following a diet that doesn't recommend balanced portions and/or doesn't include a variety of foods, you're probably putting your health at risk.

If you're trying to lose weight, don't expect it to disappear overnight. Losing weight can be a slow process—try to be patient. Don't expect to lose more than one to two pounds a week. The good news is, if you lose weight slowly and sensibly, you have a better chance of keeping it off.

Talk to your doctor. You may have seen a chart that tells you how much you "should" weigh—but everyone is different. You and your best friend may be the same height, but that doesn't mean that you'll both be healthy at the same weight. The next time you go for a checkup, talk to your doctor about your weight, and discuss your diet. She can tell you if you're on the right track.

Find hobbies that make you move. You won't build strong muscles and bones if the only part of your body that ever gets exercise is your video-game thumb. Try to balance low-energy hobbies like reading and watching movies with activities that take a little more effort. Join a

sports team, or meet up with friends to toss a Frisbee around or kick a soccer ball. Bonus: hang time with your buds, instead of veg-out time alone on the couch.

Try to get informal exercise. Experts say that exercising three times a week for ten minutes is just as effective as exercising thirty minutes all at once. That means you don't have to go to the gym to get exercise. Help out in the garden, mow the lawn, join a charity walk, bike to school, walk to the store, or take the stairs instead of the elevator at the mall. All of those little steps add up!

Make plans that don't focus on food. If you're like me, you love getting together with your friends for pizza, ice cream, or burgers. But if you find that you're spending most of your friend-time sitting across a table from your buddies, it might be time to mix things up. Go bowling, check out a fair, go to a concert or movie, take a yoga class, or just hang out at home and play games. Lunch and dinner don't have to be the only plans!

A little of this, a little of that. Don't let a brownie psych you out. It's okay to have a treat once in a while, as long as you're eating in a healthy way most of the time. Of course, the Jughead All-Burger Diet isn't the healthiest. But a side of fries now and then—just not every day!—won't kill you.

Talk to your parents. If your kitchen cupboards are filled with sugary treats and high-fat snacks, you might want to say something to your parents. Sit down with them and tell them that you're interested in healthy eating—not just for yourself, but for the rest of the family, too. Then you can all go through the kitchen together and find ways to substitute healthy foods for unhealthy ones.

Don't use food as a reward. You've aced your test, you've won your game, you've blown the competition away—it's cookie time! If this is your thinking, it's time for a mental adjustment. Same thing if you find yourself raiding the fridge at the end of a yucky day, thinking, I *deserve* to eat this quart of fudge ripple. Realize that food won't make you feel better. Call a friend, do your nails, redecorate your room, engage in an activity you enjoy, lose yourself in a hobby or craft project. You deserve it!

Don't be too hard on yourself! Hey, nobody's perfect. It's better to eat well most of the time than to try to eat "perfectly" all the time and beat yourself up when you don't. Realize that there will be times—holidays, birthdays, and so on—when you eat a little more. Just go back to your normal eating habits when the special event is over. That way, it's always easy to get back on track!

Hi, Reader!

So, there it is—now you know all about the way to look, feel, be, and do your best! We hope you liked our book.

Remember that no matter what, the most important thing is to have your best friend by your side. That's our number-one tip of all time!

Love,
Betty & Veronica